A Day with Wiggles

by Dana Catharine
illustrated by Toni Goffe

Requests for permission to make copies of any part of the work should be mailed to the following address: School Permissions, Harcourt, Inc., 6277 Sea Harbor Drive, Orlando, Florida 32887-6777.

HARCOURT and the Harcourt Logo are trademarks of Harcourt, Inc.

Printed in the United States of America

ISBN 0-15-317202-9 – A Day with Wiggles

Ordering Options
ISBN 0-15-318589-9 (Package of 5)
ISBN 0-15-316985-0 (Grade 1 Package)

2 3 4 5 6 7 8 9 10 179 02 01 00

Wiggles is my cat. What do
you think she does all day?
Most of the day, she sleeps in
my room!

1

Wiggles follows me everywhere
I go. I like to write. I try to
write about Wiggles.

2

Wiggles sits on the book I am
trying to write in today.

"Please, Wiggles," I say. "Will
you get off my book?"

Wiggles doesn't hear me, so
I move her. That cat! She moves
right back!

4

Every morning, I feed
Wiggles. Then I feed myself.
Wiggles will eat only when
I do.

5

I go out. Wiggles does, too. I go up into the big tree. Wiggles thinks about what she should do.

6

She tries to come up with me.
Then we go down. Wiggles takes
a big jump. She flies down!

The grass is full of bugs. The
bugs hop. Wiggles hops, too.

8

She tries to get the bugs, but
the bugs are too quick!

I am hungry now, so I go in.
Wiggles follows me. I get a treat
for myself. Wiggles gets a cat
treat.

10

I go to my room and take out
my book. I want to write about
what Wiggles did today.

This time, I can because
Wiggles is tired. She has gone to
sleep on my bed.

Teacher/Family Member ....

Cat Poem
Write the letters in the name *Wiggles* down the left side of a piece of paper. Have children write a word that begins with each letter to describe the cat.

 School-Home Connection
Listen as your child reads *A Day with Wiggles* to you. Ask what your child thinks was the best thing Wiggles and the boy did.

Word Count:	209

Vocabulary Words:	room
	write
	try
	please
	hear
	moved
	should
	only
	full

Phonic Elements: Long Vowel: /ē/*e, ee, ea*

she	sleeps	
me	feed	eat
tree	treat	we

....

TAKE-HOME BOOK
Welcome Home
Use with "A Bed Full of Cats."